Mog
in the dark

Judith Kerr

PictureLions
An Imprint of HarperCollins*Publishers*

For Wienitz, who saw things in the dark
that no-one else could see

First published in hardback in Great Britain
by William Collins Sons & Co. Ltd in 1983
10 9 8 7
First published in paperback in Picture Lions in 1986
and reissued in a new edition 1993
10 9 8 7
Picture Lions is an imprint of the Children's Division,
part of HarperCollins Publishers Ltd, 77-85 Fulham Palace Road,
Hammersmith, London W6 8JB
Printed and bound in Singapore by Imago

Mog sat in the dark.
Mog thought in the dark.
Mog sat in the dark
and thought dark thoughts.
Mog thought, I am here.
I am here in the dark,
but where are they?

They are all in the house.
My people are in the house.
My basket is in the house,
and my supper is in the house.
But I am not in the house.
I am here.

And
who
else
is
here
in
the
dark?

Mog thought, who is that?
Who is that in the dark?
Is that a bird?
Birds are not bad.

But it may be a big bird.

It may be a big bird with teeth.
A big bird with teeth can be bad.

Big birds with big teeth
can be bad in the dark.

Mog thought, I want my house.
Mog thought, I want my people.
Mog thought, I want my house
and my people and my basket,
and I do, I do want my supper.

Mog thought, what is that?
What is that in the dark?
Is that a mouse?
I can eat a mouse.

But it may be a big mouse.

It may be a big bad mouse.

Or it may be a dog.

There may be dogs in the dark!

They may be dogs who can climb.
Dogs who can climb can be bad.
What do dogs who can climb do?
What do they eat?
Who do they eat?

Mog thought, I do not like
dogs who can climb.
I do not want that big mouse
or the big birds with teeth.

I want my house and my people . . .

and my basket . . .

and . . . and . . . and . . .

Who? What? Where? What is that?
Who is that? Where am I?
I am up! I am up! I am up in the dark!
I am up in the dark with a thing that can fly!

Where is my house and where are my people?
And what is this thing that can fly in the dark?
Is it a bird thing? Or a mouse thing?
Or a dog thing?

"I am a mousedogbird."

A mousedogbird? What is a mousedogbird?
I do not want a mousedogbird.
I do not like this mousedogbird.
I want my house and my people and . . .

"And here they are."

Here?
"Here."
But this is a mousedogbird house
with mousedogbird people
and all mousedogbird things.

I do not want a mousedogbird basket.

And what is this supper?
I cannot eat mousedogbird supper.

This is not my house!

Mog thought, I cannot fly.

I cannot fly!

34

I cannot fly!

I cannot fly!

Or can I?

I can fly!

I can!

I can!

I can fly!

I can fly like this . . .

or like this . . .

or like that.

I can fly in the dark.

I can fly like a bird.

I am not the supper!

But who else can fly in the dark?
The big birds with teeth!

They are here in the dark!
They want supper, and who is the supper?

And here are the dogs who
can climb, and the mouse!
There is my house.
I do want my house.
But here are the birds,
and they all want supper.
What can I do? What can I do? What . . .

What?
I am not up and not in the dark!
And where are the dogs who can climb,
and the mouse, and the big birds with teeth?
They are not here. They are all not here.
But my house is here, and here are my people.

Mog thought, I am here.
I am in my house.

Not up in the dark with the mousedogbird.

I am not in the dark, and I cannot fly.

I am in my house, in my basket, with my people . . .

and I do, I do like my supper.